For Liv and Jade

This edition published by Kids Can Press in 2016

Originally published in Belgium under the title *Het prullala monster*
by Abimo Uitgeverij

Illustrations by Jacques Maes and Lise Braekers

English translation © 2016 Kids Can Press

Kids Can Press acknowledges the financial support of the
Government of Ontario, through the Ontario Media Development
Corporation's Ontario Book Initiative.

Published in Canada by
Kids Can Press Ltd.
25 Dockside Drive
Toronto, ON M5A 0B5

Published in the U.S. by
Kids Can Press Ltd.
2250 Military Road
Tonawanda, NY 14150

www.kidscanpress.com

English edition edited by Yvette Ghione
Designed by Jacques Maes and Lise Braekers

This book is smyth sewn casebound.
Manufactured in Malaysia in 3/2016 by Tien Wah Press (Pte.) Ltd.

CM 16 0 9 8 7 6 5 4 3 2 1

Library and Archives Canada Cataloguing in Publication

Mulders, Jean-Paul, 1968—
[Prullala monster. English]
   The Pruwahaha monster / written by Jean-Paul Mulders ;
illustrated by Jacques Maes and Lise Braekers.

Translation of: Het Prullala monster.
ISBN 978-1-77138-566-4 (hardback)

   I. Maes, Jacques, illustrator II. Braekers, Lise, illustrator
III. Title. IV. Title: Prullala monster. English

PZ7.M88Pr 2016   j839.313'7   C2016-900000-1

Kids Can Press is a ɭOᴦᴜꜱ™ Entertainment company

THE
pruwahaha
MONSTER

Written by **Jean-Paul Mulders**
Illustrated by **Jacques Maes** & **Lise Braekers**

Kids Can Press

Once upon a time, there was a little boy who loved
to swing. His father always took him to swing on the
same swing near the farmhouse with the green doors
where the ladies who made pancakes lived.

What the little boy
did not know was that a
monster lurked near the farmhouse.
The monster lived in a cottage
with orange shingles and
a door with a bolt.

The cottage was small but
the monster was *huuuuuge*.
The neighbors hadn't a clue it could
open the door by sliding the latch
up with a single CLAW.

One year, when the little boy was just five,
the monster overslept. Usually it woke in
the spring, when the birds made their nests.
But that year, the monster was startled to
find it had woken in the autumn — there
was already a chill in the air.

And it was VERY hungry.

Carefully pushing open the door of its little
cottage, the monster poked out its dirty
snout and let out a snort —

Pfffffffffffffffffffffffffffffrrt!

A puff of smoke escaped from between the
monster's teeth. It smelled of sprouts and
old slippers.

The monster said, "I can smell children."
And there was only one thing the monster
liked to eat.
It did not like cookies.
It did not like licorice.
It did not like chocolate.
It did not like jawbreakers.
It did not even like spaghetti and meatballs.

The only thing the monster liked to eat was ...
little children. The monster thought they
were delicious.

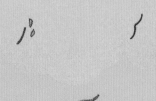

The monster flared its nostrils wide. The monster
could SMELL little feet and little hands and rosy little
cheeks ... but it could not SEE children anywhere.
It could see a bicycle.
It could see an oak tree, and acorns on the ground.
It could see an apple core.
It could see a scampering cat.
It could see the white streak of an airplane in the sky.
It could see a bird pooping from its perch.

But it could NOT see a child.

The monster lumbered along. Its tail swished around and its teeth flashed in the late afternoon sun. The monster peered over the warts on its nose and suddenly it saw ... a little child!

The child was playing on a swing.
The monster thought, *YUMMY!*

Step by step, it crept closer. It had especially
sneaky feet with suckers for extra grip.
Closer and closer the monster crept while
the little boy kept swinging.

Back and forth
and back and forth
and back and forth
the little boy swung,
laughing away.

All the while, the monster thought,
as quietly as only monsters can think.
I'm going to gobble up that child.

The monster tensed its
muscles and sinews.
It held its breath.
It turned its tongue round
seven times in its mouth
the way monsters do when
they are out hunting. And then
it leaped out and howled:
Prruwwwahhahahaha!

But what was this?
The little boy did not even blink. No ...
He laughed! And he kept swinging.
Back and forth.
As if nothing had happened.

I cannot believe my eyes,
the monster thought.

This
is
not
possible.

This
is
too
preposterous
for
words.

But the monster was stubborn.

"I must be out of practice," it growled.

"I will try again."

It hissed like a steam iron. It rolled its eyes.

With every ounce of strength it had in its body,

it bashed its tail on the ground and roared:

Prruwwahahahaaaa!

Spit smelling of cauliflower and sweaty socks
dribbled from its mouth.

But still the little boy did not jump in fright.
He kept laughing, even harder this time.

This made the monster terribly sad.
It stole away, its tail between its legs.
"I've lost the knack," it rumbled.
"I am an old relic. Children are no longer
afraid of me. I leap out at them and I act
mean, and it only makes them laugh."
(The monster said that last word very
quietly because it was embarrassed.)

It slunk back to its little cottage on its sneaky, suckered feet. Someone had raked leaves into a neat pile in front of the door. The monster tried some. The leaves tasted dirty, and crunched between its teeth. But the monster kept eating, because it was ravenous. It dipped the leaves in a mud-and-nettle sauce.

When all of its stomachs were full, the monster went inside. It put its head in its paws and had a good grumble. Then the monster fell asleep and dreamed of little children who were still afraid of old-fashioned monsters.

And no one knows whether the Pruwahaha Monster
woke up again the following spring …

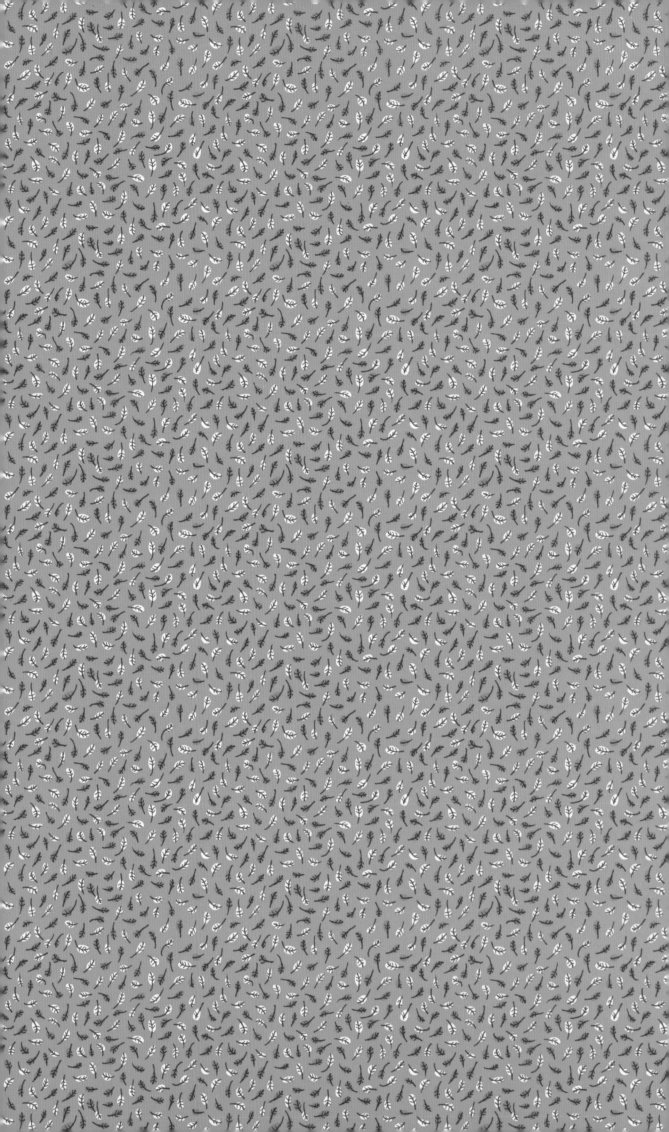